Also by Andi Michelson

The Baxter School Kids: Queen Bea

Table of Contents

What If?
A Worrier's Toolkit

PUBLIC SCHOOL EDITION

Andi Michelson

Foreword

Martin L. Michelson, MA, LCPC, NCC

Have you ever felt stressed out about what's going on in your world with family, friends, school, health or other things? Was it difficult to focus on what you were feeling, or how to handle it, or who to talk to because you were worried? Guess what? You're not alone in this.

Many of us spend a lot of time, energy, and emotion being anxious and worrying about life and all its issues. We want to solve the problem(s), or find some answers, or just move on from the doubts, nervousness, and troubles.

A Worrier's Toolkit may be able to help you. It includes some exercises for you to think through your concerns and uncertainties, puts them in perspective, and offers some ideas to help you move on.

Good luck, and remember: "Don't sweat the small stuff."

Note to Parents...

This book is intended to help kids feel prepared and safe. Working through these exercises—either alone or with your assistance—empowers children by helping them think through some difficult scenarios ahead of time. As they write down positive actions they can take, it helps them to develop a plan with multiple options and to be decisive if the need arises.

They can approach life from a position of strength, rather than one of fear.

If this seems to be stressing out your child more, you may choose to set aside the workbook until a later time. You can reassure them that most things we worry about never even happen. And when they do, they are usually not as catastrophic as we imagine.

In Case of an Emergency...

My Address: _____

_____

Parent's Name and Phone Number: _____

_____

Parent's Place of Employment: _____

_____

Parent's Name and Phone Number: _____

_____

Parent's Place of Employment: _____

_____

Other Caregiver's Name and Phone Number:

_____

Doctor's Name and Phone Number: _____

_____

If You Need to Call 9-1-1...

Take a deep breath and stay calm.

Often the dispatcher's first question will be, "What is your emergency?" Tell them if you need medical, fire, or police.

Give your location as best you can. If you don't know the address, give the street or cross-street or what businesses are nearby.

Give your phone number. This way, if the call gets dropped, the dispatcher will call you back.

Answer any questions the dispatcher asks. They might ask what happened, how many people are involved, their condition, etc.

Stay on the phone until they say you may hang up.

Introduction

Are you a worrier?

Do you worry a lot?

Do you ever worry you are wasting your life by worrying so much?

It's true that most of the things you worry about NEVER EVEN HAPPEN.

But knowing that doesn't seem to help you.

Instead, when you start to worry about something, you can ask yourself two things:

1. WHAT IS THE WORST THING THAT CAN HAPPEN?

2. WHAT POSITIVE ACTIONS CAN I TAKE?

Think of this as PLANNING AHEAD. And then you can quit thinking about it!

On the following pages, we can practice this together. You will see a potential problem (remember: this may never even happen to you!). There will be space for you to write down the VERY WORST THING that could happen. Then write down some actions you can take. Don't turn the page until you come up with some ideas! Additional possible solutions will be on the next page. You get to choose your own action plan.

This is your book...

Unless it is a library book.

Uh-oh! Did you write in a library book?

(Let's do a little practice here...)

WHAT IF I write in a library book?

WHAT IS THE WORST THING THAT COULD HAPPEN?

_____

_____

_____

_____

WHAT POSITIVE ACTIONS CAN I TAKE?

_____

_____

_____

_____

WHAT IF I write in a library book?

WHAT IS THE WORST THING THAT COULD HAPPEN?

I will get in trouble and have to pay for the book.

WHAT POSITIVE ACTIONS CAN I TAKE?

I can try to erase my answers.

I can apologize.

I can pay for the book with my allowance. Besides, it's a good book that I'd like to keep anyways!

One final thought...Worriers tend to be creative people; after all, we imagine all sorts of crazy things. Try to harness that creative energy in a positive way!

School & Social Situations

WHAT IF I forget to bring my lunch to school?

WHAT IS THE WORST THING THAT COULD HAPPEN?

_____

_____

_____

_____

WHAT POSITIVE ACTIONS CAN I TAKE?

_____

_____

_____

_____

WHAT IF I forget to bring my lunch to school?

HERE ARE SOME POSITIVE ACTIONS I CAN TAKE...

Use my electronic account to buy lunch.

Accept half a sandwich or granola bar from my friend.

Call my parents to see if they can bring my lunch.

Know that even though I might feel very hungry, no one ever died from missing one meal!

WHAT IF I say something really stupid in front of everyone?

WHAT IS THE WORST THING THAT COULD HAPPEN?

_____

_____

_____

_____

WHAT POSITIVE ACTIONS CAN I TAKE?

_____

_____

_____

_____

WHAT IF I say something really stupid in front of everyone?

HERE ARE SOME POSITIVE ACTIONS I CAN TAKE...

Laugh at myself!

Realize that everyone does embarrassing things sometimes.

WHAT IF no one likes me?

WHAT IS THE WORST THING THAT COULD HAPPEN?

_____

_____

_____

_____

WHAT POSITIVE ACTIONS CAN I TAKE?

_____

_____

_____

_____

WHAT IF no one likes me?

HERE ARE SOME POSITIVE ACTIONS I CAN TAKE...

Do a reality check: is there really no one who likes me? What about my parents and siblings, my grandparents, teachers, neighbors, pets?

Understand that not everyone likes everyone! Don't I have certain people that I enjoy more than others?

Be genuinely interested in other people.

Develop hobbies and skills that will give meaning to my life and help me make connections with others who have similar interests.

WHAT IF I forget to do my homework?

WHAT IS THE WORST THING THAT COULD HAPPEN?

_____

_____

_____

_____

WHAT POSITIVE ACTIONS CAN I TAKE?

_____

_____

_____

_____

WHAT IF I forget to do my homework?

HERE ARE SOME POSITIVE ACTIONS I CAN TAKE...

Ask the teacher if I can have one more day to finish it.

Offer to do extra work for extra credit.

Think about my time management. What did I do instead of my homework? Did I watch TV or play with friends before completing my work?

Put the homework in my backpack as soon as I finish it, so I won't forget to take it to school.

WHAT IF I fail a test?

WHAT IS THE WORST THING THAT COULD HAPPEN?

_____

_____

_____

_____

WHAT POSITIVE ACTIONS CAN I TAKE?

_____

_____

_____

_____

WHAT IF I fail a test?

HERE ARE SOME POSITIVE ACTIONS I CAN TAKE...

Ask the teacher if I can do extra credit to bring my grade back up.

Resolve to be prepared the next time!

Ask for help from a trusted adult or seek tutoring.

WHAT IF my new haircut turns out all wrong?

WHAT IS THE WORST THING THAT COULD HAPPEN?

_____

_____

_____

_____

WHAT POSITIVE ACTIONS CAN I TAKE?

_____

_____

_____

WHAT IF my new haircut turns out all wrong?

HERE ARE SOME POSITIVE ACTIONS I CAN TAKE...

Ask my friends and family for input; maybe it's not as bad as I think.

It IS as bad as I think! Ask the hairdresser to cut some more off into a different style.

~~Put a paper bag over my head and stay home for six weeks.~~

Focus on letting my inner beauty shine.

Remember: hair always grows. This is temporary.

WHAT IF I'm late for practice?

WHAT IS THE WORST THING THAT COULD HAPPEN?

_____

_____

_____

_____

WHAT POSITIVE ACTIONS CAN I TAKE?

_____

_____

_____

_____

WHAT IF I'm late for practice?

HERE ARE SOME POSITIVE ACTIONS I CAN TAKE...

Apologize to the coach and the rest of the team.

I can give the reason, but I won't make excuses.

Work extra hard to make up for it.

Plan better next time so I can be on time.

Just a Note...

A **reason** is a logical explanation for an action. Examining your reasons for doing something encourages understanding, accepts responsibility and allows for improvement in the future.

An **excuse** is an attempt to defend your actions. It can include blaming others, trying to make yourself look good, or avoiding consequences.

WHAT IF the teacher doesn't like me?

WHAT IS THE WORST THING THAT COULD HAPPEN?

_____

_____

_____

_____

WHAT POSITIVE ACTIONS CAN I TAKE?

_____

_____

_____

_____

WHAT IF the teacher doesn't like me?

HERE ARE SOME POSITIVE ACTIONS I CAN TAKE...

Do a reality check; consider if the teacher doesn't like me, or is just pushing me to do my best.

Think about my behavior. Can I apologize for something I did that might have upset the teacher?

Be helpful.

If the teacher is truly being mean to me specifically, talk to a parent or another teacher.

Realize that I will encounter difficult people throughout my life.

Try my best. Being kind and doing my best are what I have control over.

WHAT IF kids laugh at me?

WHAT IS THE WORST THING THAT COULD HAPPEN?

_____

_____

_____

_____

WHAT POSITIVE ACTIONS CAN I TAKE?

_____

_____

_____

_____

WHAT IF kids laugh at me?

HERE ARE SOME POSITIVE ACTIONS I CAN TAKE...

If they are not truly being mean, I can choose to laugh along with them.

I can remember what it feels like to be laughed at if I am ever tempted to laugh at someone else.

I can focus on doing the things that make me special and do them well.

I can become a friend to someone else.

I can talk to a friend or trusted adult to get it off my chest.

WHAT IF my coach doesn't put me in the game?

WHAT IS THE WORST THING THAT COULD HAPPEN?

_____

_____

_____

_____

WHAT POSITIVE ACTIONS CAN I TAKE?

_____

_____

_____

_____

WHAT IF my coach doesn't put me in the game?

HERE ARE SOME POSITIVE ACTIONS I CAN TAKE...

At my next practice, ask my coach if there are specific skills I need to improve.

Work harder at practice.

Practice more on my own.

Support my teammates by being positive and cheering them on.

WHAT IF I see someone being bullied?

WHAT IS THE WORST THING THAT COULD HAPPEN?

_____

_____

_____

_____

WHAT POSITIVE ACTIONS CAN I TAKE?

_____

_____

_____

_____

WHAT IF I see someone being bullied?

HERE ARE SOME POSITIVE ACTIONS I CAN TAKE...

Tell the bully to stop.

Make sure I don't ever go along with bullying.

Be a friend to that person, if possible.

Encourage others to think what it would feel like to get picked on.

Ask a teacher or other adult for help.

WHAT IF a shooter comes into our school?

WHAT IS THE WORST THING THAT COULD HAPPEN?

_____

_____

_____

_____

WHAT POSITIVE ACTIONS CAN I TAKE?

_____

_____

_____

_____

WHAT IF a shooter comes into our school?

HERE ARE SOME POSITIVE ACTIONS I CAN TAKE...

First, follow the instructions of my teacher or other trusted school officials. Follow the plan that my class has practiced in active shooter drills.

If no adult is present, run to safety! Escaping is the best choice, if I can do it.

If I can't escape, hiding is the next best thing. I can lock or barricade doors.

Fight back if I can't escape or hide.

Just a Note...

When shootings happen in schools, it understandably is all over the news. But it is actually a very rare occurrence. It is very unlikely that you will ever be in this situation.

Friends

WHAT IF my best friend likes somebody else better?

WHAT IS THE WORST THING THAT COULD HAPPEN?

_____

_____

_____

_____

WHAT POSITIVE ACTIONS CAN I TAKE?

_____

_____

_____

_____

WHAT IF my best friend likes somebody else better?

HERE ARE SOME POSITIVE ACTIONS I CAN TAKE...

Continue to be friendly to them both.

If I'm feeling jealous, tell my friend privately and kindly. Try to work through my negative feelings; nobody likes a jealous friend!

Be open to new friendships.

Remember to be myself, even if someone doesn't like me.

WHAT IF my family moves to a new town?

WHAT IS THE WORST THING THAT COULD HAPPEN?

_____

_____

_____

_____

WHAT POSITIVE ACTIONS CAN I TAKE?

_____

_____

_____

_____

WHAT IF my family moves to a new town?

HERE ARE SOME POSITIVE ACTIONS I CAN TAKE...

Keep in touch with my old friends (video calls, phone, email, snail mail, occasional visits).

Look at it as an adventure! Or a fresh start!

Reach out to make new friends.

Join sports, clubs, band or other activities in my new place to meet kids who share my interests.

Write down my thoughts and feelings in a journal.

Family

WHAT IF my parent loses his or her job?

WHAT IS THE WORST THING THAT COULD HAPPEN?

_____

_____

_____

_____

WHAT POSITIVE ACTIONS CAN I TAKE?

_____

_____

_____

_____

WHAT IF my parent loses his or her job?

HERE ARE SOME POSITIVE ACTIONS I CAN TAKE...

Talk to my parent (or another adult) about my fears.

Ask my parent how we can work together as a family through this time.

Realize that temporarily we might have to spend money on just the basics, rather than on the extras.

See if I can work for spending money.

WHAT IF my pet dies?

WHAT IS THE WORST THING THAT COULD HAPPEN?

_____

_____

_____

_____

WHAT POSITIVE ACTIONS CAN I TAKE?

_____

_____

_____

_____

WHAT IF my pet dies?

HERE ARE SOME POSITIVE ACTIONS I CAN TAKE...

Give him one last cuddle.

Have a memorial service.

Frame a photo of myself playing with her.

Write a poem or story about the fun times we had.

Realize that someday I may choose to love another pet, and that's okay.
Even though it won't replace the one I lost, it can bring me joy again.

WHAT IF my parents argue?

WHAT IS THE WORST THING THAT COULD HAPPEN?

_____

_____

_____

_____

WHAT POSITIVE ACTIONS CAN I TAKE?

_____

_____

_____

_____

WHAT IF my parents argue?

HERE ARE SOME POSITIVE ACTIONS I CAN TAKE...

Love them both.

Go visit a friend if I'm allowed to.

Find a teacher, counselor or religious leader to talk with.

Listen to music.

Know it's okay to cry. This is scary and upsetting, but I know I can get through it.

WHAT IF my family member gets sick or dies?

WHAT IS THE WORST THING THAT COULD HAPPEN?

_____

_____

_____

_____

WHAT POSITIVE ACTIONS CAN I TAKE?

_____

_____

_____

_____

WHAT IF my family member gets sick or dies?

HERE ARE SOME POSITIVE ACTIONS I CAN TAKE...

Cry if I feel like it.

Remember and write down happy memories of things we did together.

Share my feelings with other family members.

Be thankful for the time we had.

Do something in his or her memory (plant a tree, write a story, sing or play a song, raise money for charity).

Live my life, embracing the parts of "me" I inherited from him or her, knowing they would want me to be happy.

Emergency, Safety, & Health

WHAT IF I get lost?

WHAT IS THE WORST THING THAT COULD HAPPEN?

_____

_____

_____

WHAT POSITIVE ACTIONS CAN I TAKE?

_____

_____

_____

WHAT IF I get lost?

HERE ARE SOME POSITIVE ACTIONS I CAN TAKE...

Stop and look around to see if anything looks familiar.

Ask a safe person for help (a police officer or someone who works where I'm lost).

Use my cell phone (or borrow one) to call my family.

Don't leave with someone I don't know.

Just a Note...

If you're lost, NEVER leave with someone you don't know.
Most people are safe, but leaving can make it harder to
find your family.

WHAT IF I hear someone say they are going to hurt themself or others?

WHAT IS THE WORST THING THAT COULD HAPPEN?

_____

_____

_____

_____

WHAT POSITIVE ACTIONS CAN I TAKE?

_____

_____

_____

_____

WHAT IF I hear someone say they are going to hurt themself or others?

HERE ARE SOME POSITIVE ACTIONS I CAN TAKE...

Get away as quickly as it's safe to do so.

Tell an adult.

If the first person I tell doesn't believe me or do anything about it, keep telling other adults until I can find help.

Know that if someone hurts themself or others it is not my fault.

WHAT IF I get a horrible disease?

WHAT IS THE WORST THING THAT COULD HAPPEN?

_____

_____

_____

_____

WHAT POSITIVE ACTIONS CAN I TAKE?

_____

_____

_____

_____

WHAT IF I get a horrible disease?

HERE ARE SOME POSITIVE ACTIONS I CAN TAKE...

Learn as much as I can about the disease.

Talk to other people who are living with it.

Ask the doctor what I can do to stay as healthy as possible.

Continue to be physically active in the ways I still can.

WHAT IF I wake up and smell smoke?

WHAT IS THE WORST THING THAT COULD HAPPEN?

_____

_____

_____

_____

WHAT POSITIVE ACTIONS CAN I TAKE?

_____

_____

_____

_____

Ahead of Time...

1. Make a family plan of a safe place to meet.
2. Ask my parents if we can do fire drills.
3. Ask my parents to maintain working smoke alarms.

WHAT IF I wake up and smell smoke?

IN CASE OF FIRE...

Yell to others who are in the house to alert them.

Get out of the house immediately. If my door is closed, feel it; if it's hot or I see smoke coming under the door, I'll need to escape through the window.

If the smoke is thick, I can crawl on the floor where the air is clearer.

If my clothes catch fire—STOP-DROP-ROLL; this will smother the flames.

Dial 911 after I'm safely outside.

Don't try to take things with me or go back inside for anything. The firefighters will work hard to save what they can and make sure everyone is safe.

WHAT IF someone touches me in an inappropriate way?

WHAT IS THE WORST THING THAT COULD HAPPEN?

_____

_____

_____

_____

WHAT POSITIVE ACTIONS CAN I TAKE?

_____

_____

_____

_____

WHAT IF someone touches me in an inappropriate way?

WHAT I CAN DO...

Tell them 'NO' in a loud voice.

Get away if I can.

Tell a trusted adult as soon as I can.

Know that it is NOT my fault.

WHAT IF we get in a car accident?

WHAT IS THE WORST THING THAT COULD HAPPEN?

_____

_____

_____

WHAT POSITIVE ACTIONS CAN I TAKE?

_____

_____

_____

WHAT IF we get in a car accident?

IN CASE OF AN ACCIDENT...

Call 911.

Don't move someone unless they are more likely to be injured by staying there.

Stop any bleeding by applying pressure.

Follow instructions given by police, fire or ambulance crews.

Just a Note...

1. Always wear a seat belt!
2. Take a basic first aid class and keep a first aid kit in the car.
3. Talk to my parents about keeping a hammer or emergency device under the seat in case I need to break a window to escape.

WHAT IF we have a tornado/hurricane/earthquake?

WHAT IS THE WORST THING THAT COULD HAPPEN?

_____

_____

_____

_____

WHAT POSITIVE ACTIONS CAN I TAKE?

_____

_____

_____

_____

WHAT IF we have a tornado/hurricane/earthquake?

IN CASE OF AN ACCIDENT...

Stay calm.

Listen to the radio for safety instructions.

Ahead of Time:

1. Take a basic first aid class.
2. Make a kit of emergency supplies: food, water, flashlight, batteries, radio, whistle.
3. Make a family plan of where to meet if we get separated from each other.
4. Create a list of phone numbers of relatives and friends.

Here are some extra practice pages for you to write down things that you worry about. After you think them through, you may want to talk with an adult to get another perspective.

WHAT IF

?

_____

WHAT IS THE WORST THING THAT COULD HAPPEN?

_____

_____

_____

WHAT POSITIVE ACTIONS CAN I TAKE?

_____

_____

_____

WHAT IF

?

WHAT IS THE WORST THING THAT COULD HAPPEN?

_____

_____

_____

WHAT POSITIVE ACTIONS CAN I TAKE?

_____

_____

_____

WHAT IF

?

___

WHAT IS THE WORST THING THAT COULD HAPPEN?

_____

_____

_____

_____

WHAT POSITIVE ACTIONS CAN I TAKE?

_____

_____

_____

_____

WHAT IF

?

WHAT IS THE WORST THING THAT COULD HAPPEN?

_____

_____

_____

_____

WHAT POSITIVE ACTIONS CAN I TAKE?

_____

_____

_____

_____

Acknowledgments

Many thanks to my editor, Rachel DiScipio Ketler, facilitator of the Writers of the Round Table writing group at Massillon Public Library, for designing the cover and helping to demystify the whole self-publishing process.

I am greatly indebted to Dr. Melissa D., Sarah Downes, Martin L. Michelson, and Erin Pittman, the mental health professionals who reviewed this manuscript and shared their insights.

All my love and appreciation to my husband, Chris Beebe, for believing in me.

And my eternal gratitude to my Lord, Jesus Christ, who calms the seas.

About the Author

Andi Michelson is a children's author. In writing picture books and chapter books, she explores nature, farm life, and relationships.

When she's not writing or teaching children and adults in her piano studio, Andi can usually be found chasing chickens, walking in the woods with her goats, or getting dirt under her fingernails in the garden. She lives in Northeast Ohio with her husband and various farm animals.